FLAWLESS

J. SCOTT COATSWORTH

Copyright © 2024 by J. Scott Coatsworth

All rights reserved.

No part of this book may be reproduced or transmitted in any form or by any means, electronic or mechanical, except for the purpose of review and/or reference, without explicit permission in writing from the publisher.

Cover artwork design © 2024 by J. Scott Coatsworth and Sleepy Fox Studio
sleepyfoxstudio.net

Published by Water Dragon Publishing
waterdragonpublishing.com

ISBN 978-1-962538-76-3 (Trade Paperback)

FIRST EDITION

10 9 8 7 6 5 4 3 2 1

FLAWLESS

I GUIDED THE *SWALLOW* along the surface of Eros, my ship locked in a perfect dance with her, turning with her like Fred Astaire with Ginger Rogers on the old *flatties* from a couple of centuries ago. My chipped black nail-polished fingers moved the joystick flawlessly, firing the attitude jets a little here, a little there to match 433 Eros's spin.

The other wildcatters back on Ceres gave me shit about the polish. "Guys don't color their nails." *Especially* rough and tumble asteroid prospectors. Like anyone ought to care what you did out here, in the vastness of space.

Half of them had tattoos of flowers with women's names on their asses. I knew. I'd seen them in the showers. *And they give a shit about my nail polish?*

Valeriana — my drag patron — would have told them all to fuck off. Me, I'm a *get-along* kinda guy. I'd say that it helps protect my cuticles from radiation, but I doubt they know what cuticles are.

Flawless

"Grayson Eck, captain of the *White Swallow*, picking up the last can before returning to Ceres."

Rosie's voice purred through the ship's speakers. "Acknowledged, *Captain Awesome*."

I grinned. It was our own private joke. I was a sucker for old cartoon *flatties*, though the ship mind's voice was a bit more butch than the Jetsons version.

Rosie would append the date and time info to the log in *Ceres Standard*, synched to UTC back on Earth.

I always felt stupid recording the logs. Not the talking to myself part — wildcatters did that a lot out here in the middle of nowhere — but the narrating every move bit. But the Belt Patrol requires them for damage assessment in case there's a *major incident*. Which basically means if your ship blows itself to smithereens. And those BP fuckers could make your life hell if you didn't follow the rules.

I passed over the old *Near Earth Asteroid Rendezvous - Shoemaker* mission, its four square panels covered in fine dust, likely kicked up when the little craft landed on this forlorn piece of real estate that spent much of its life far away from the shipping lanes between Earth and Mars. I was surprised no one had scooped it up for salvage, but then again, we 'catters have an almost supernatural fear of abandoned ships.

Eros tumbled slowly beneath the *Swallow*, sometimes resembling one of those primitive clay carvings of a horse, and sometimes a squished boomerang. I wasn't the first one to mine her. She's close enough to Earth and Mars, depending on their own eccentric dance, that she's been visited at least half a dozen times. But I had better equipment, thanks to Valeriana's money.

As I passed over Psyche Crater, I saw the remains of some of those earlier missions, open void mines where the asteroid regolith was scraped away *en masse* to mine aluminum from the substrate, leaving ugly scars on the otherwise pristine asteroid's surface.

I chuckled. *Pristine, if you ignore a few billion years of mother void's bombardment.*

I was here for the platinum, something far rarer than aluminum, and far harder to harvest. One last pick-up to make, and then I'd head back to Ceres to find a buyer.

There. On the horizon, a light flashed, red against the near-monochrome sparkling of a hundred million stars. I grinned. My smile turned to a frown as I read the data coming in from the beacon. Something was off. It was only two-thirds full, and a smattering of drones were still waiting to unload their scores. "Rosie, what's going on with that can?"

"Checking, Cap."

I guided the *Swallow* over the rocky terrain with practiced ease. I could leave it to the ship mind — most 'catters do. But I'm also a *hands-on* kinda guy.

"There's some problem with the loading chute."

"Slag it." This would throw off my schedule. I had six hours to get the can and set off for Ceres before the math made the transit next to impossible with my remaining fuel. I always cut it close, but this time I might have just fucked myself over, and damned good.

The can sat in a shallow crater, where the near-constant shadow would make it harder for pirates to find — the red light only came on when I was in close proximity.

I nudged the *Swallow* toward the crater rim, urging the ship down onto the rough surface with a series of short bursts. She settled down neatly on the crater's edge, far enough back not to risk a landslide, and dug her claws into the Erotian soil.

I said a quick prayer to Mother Void for her safety — if I lost her, I was truly screwed — the closest registered ship was a few million kilometers away. And Rosie would be none too happy about it either.

I climbed into my suit and Valeriana's music pumped into my ears as soon as I activated the pressurization system, a deep-thromb beat layered with her own lyrics. I dialed it back to a reasonable level that wouldn't melt my eardrums as I checked the suit for leaks.

Feet firm on the ground
A swirl of stars above me
Waiting for the sound
Hoping you really love me ...

Not her best work, but hey, it paid the bills, including the new drones.

Satisfied that the suit seals would hold, I climbed down into the airlock, crouching inside as the lid closed above me.

In the *tridee* shows, airlocks are always expansive things, wide enough to stretch your arms and not touch both sides. In reality, mass is weight, and weight is fuel. Most of the wildcatter ships I'd been on had "canister locks" like mine, small spaces that minimized the air and time needed to cycle in and out. Mine was barely bigger than I was, and the air hissed out in a matter of seconds.

"Stay safe out there, Cap." Rosie's voice sounded tinny over my suit speakers.

"Hold down the fort." I knew she'd do more than that — Rosie could get the ship home without me, if it ever came to that. *What would it take to get her to abandon my old wildcatter ass?*

The airlock elevator lowered me out of the ship to the surface, exposing me to the cold of the hard void.

My suit heater kicked in, keeping me warm enough as I searched for the guide line that led down into the crater.

My landing was flawless, putting me just a few feet away from the cable that sparkled with energy absorbed from the sun every time this side of Eros passes her shining face.

I frowned. The high-strength cable had been a gift from Archer, five years earlier, before he'd been taken away from me. You never took life in space for granted. It could be snatched away from you in an instant.

I pushed away the memory and the spasm of pain that accompanied it. There was work to do.

With a flick of my wrist, my boots extended their own claws into the asteroid regolith. I began the careful trek across the broken surface. Eros had some gravity, but it was unevenly distributed, and it would be easy enough to push off too hard and send myself sailing into the void.

Someone told me once that Australia was full of poisonous animals, and that everything there could kill you — though I wasn't sure if that applied to koalas and kangaroos. Well, space is like that too. Everything can kill you, and it only takes one misstep to write yourself a ticket to a rendezvous with Mother Void and the space graveyard.

I reached the cable, my hand closing around it, and used it to guide myself down into the crater. I'd placed it there when I'd left the can, a couple of weeks before. When I left, I'd uproot the tall stakes it was suspended on and bring them all back to the ship.

Flawless

I slipped over the shallow rim of the crater and let myself down step by step until I reached the semi-flat floor, and turned carefully to see what was wrong with the can. "Holy fucking void."

A body lay next to the can, which lay on its side, blocking loading chute access for the drones.

Somebody tried to steal my stash. I crossed the intervening space, hand over hand on the line, and knelt to check the person's suit. It was standard issue — the kind they give space tourists — and it was still humming, its solar panels picking up enough juice to keep its occupant, if not exactly warm, then warm enough.

I turned the body over — a feat more difficult than it sounds when you're using one hand to hold a guide line and trying not to throw yourself into space. Luckily — for me and for them — they'd tethered themselves to the can, or they might have been thrown off when my booby trap had detonated. Their suit visor was covered with dust.

I wiped it with the back of my glove, exposing the face beneath, and whistled. The sun was just rising over the edge of Eros, giving me a good look at his face.

He was young, maybe twenty — a good twenty years younger than me. And handsome. Fresh up from Mars or Earth, I'd reckon, looking to make his first score. He reminded me of that good looking kid in the *tridees* set on Venus, the one who was a real asshole, but everyone loved him anyhow … Vim Vasser, that's what they called him. *Like Venus would ever be habitable …*

"Fucking idiot." I ought to leave him there to die, or better yet, fling him out into the void where no one would ever find him.

J. Scott Coatsworth

The would-be pirate was lucky — the blast should have blown a hole in his suit. I put off the decision about what to do with "Vim," determined to fix my own situation first. Time was flying by.

I clipped my own tether onto the last spike and reached down to lift the can back to an upright position.

The damned thing didn't want to budge. Platinum is heavy, and even if things are essentially weightless in this micro-grav environment, they still have mass.

Frowning, I reached for my best piece of space technology — the crowbar I kept next to the wrench on my belt. The two tools had gotten me out of more problems than I could count on the fingers of both hands — and probably on my toes too.

The little digger drones watched expectantly, little black crab-like things that clung to pieces of regolith. Once I exposed the loading chute, they could return inside with their hauls.

Wedging it under the can, I strained to lift it a few inches, sweating inside the suit, never a pleasant experience. My enviro controls kicked it up a notch, cooling me off and sucking the water from my skin.

Still it resisted me, staying stubbornly in position.

I pushed harder, straining my muscles, groaning at the effort.

All at once it gave, shifting enough to expose the loading chute hole in the side of the can and throwing me backward. My arms windmilled as I tried to stop my sudden ascension into the starry void.

Don't panic. Archer's voice came to me. *Fear kills more wildcatters than accidents.* I closed my eyes and let my arms fall slack at my side, waiting for the inevitable.

Flawless

I miss you, Arch.

A sharp tug stopped my upward motion as the slack in the tether I'd connected to the can ran out. Thank the void it had enough mass — and was secured well enough — enough to handle my weight.

With a quick prayer of thanks, I grasped the carbon fiber cable and I pulled myself back to the asteroid's surface again, hand over hand, shivering at the close call. I let out a sigh of relief as my feet touched down on the rough soil with a crunch I could feel in my bones.

Time to deal with my uninvited visitor.

I unclipped my tether and reconnected it to the cord that ran up to the ship, and then undid the intruder's tether and attached it to my belt. He weighed a hell of a lot less than the can. I ought to be able to haul him up the short slope and get him to the *Swallow*.

I contacted the ship. "Rosie, we've got a pirate out here."

"You in trouble, Cap?" Her voice sounded concerned, and I wondered — not for the first time — how close she was to sentient.

"Nope, all under control. It's just a kid, and he's unconscious. Bringing him in ... wanna heat things up a little in there?"

"Got it." Rosie was good at her job. She'd have things ready when we arrived.

Careful not to launch myself into space again, I knelt next to the handsome stranger and lifted him into the air. I decided I could use one of the suit's handles to carry him like a floating suitcase. Whenever I let him go, the young man's body would ever so slowly drift back to the ground.

I made my way back up the crater's slope, sending mini avalanches of dirt and rocks streaming down behind me, bit**s** of them floating up toward the stars to sparkle in the void as they caught glints of sunlight.

Using the cord as my guide, I nudged my human luggage along step by step.

I did some quick calculations in my head. If I was careful, I'd have enough food for two, until I could haul his sorry ass back to Ceres. Water might be a bit tighter, but it could be recycled.

Then I'd find out who "Vim" really was, and get his company or sponsors to pay me for the trouble.

I grinned. *I might even come out a bit ahead.*

The rim of the crater proved the most difficult. I couldn't simultaneously climb over the top and hold on to my human cargo. So I set him down on a wide rock and scrambled up over the lip, trusting him to stay where he was.

I turned to find him slowly drifting away, down the slope.

"Dammit." I braced myself and tugged on the tether that connected us, arresting his downward motion, and pulled him back up toward me. Poor kid might have bumped into a couple of rocks on the way up, but his suit seals held, so I considered it a win.

In another five minutes, I had him stuffed inside the ship's small airlock, rising up into the guts of the *Swallow*. Once he was inside and the airlock was pressurized, I'd programmed the lift to dump him out onto the floor. He'd be okay in there until I could get back down to the can and hitch it up to the ship's hydraulic system. Then we'd be good to go. "Rosie, I have that bit of human cargo for you. Keep an eye on him?"

Flawless

"Got it, Cap. Friend or foe?"

"Foe. I think." I snorted. "Hell if I know." I checked the time. I'd lost an hour, but as long as nothing else happened to slow me down, we'd launch in plenty of time to reach Ceres.

Funny, that word we. Until very recently, it had meant the ship and me. Here I'd been, all lonely, and *this* was what Mother Void chose to send me.

I shook my head. The universe had a weird sense of humor.

• • •

An hour later, I had the can hooked up to the ship's winch and the last of the digger drones sealed inside with their precious cargo. One hadn't returned. It wasn't that unusual — the belt was as dangerous a place for mechs as it was for us fleshy beasts.

I climbed the slope for what I hoped was the last time, looking forward to a hot steam shower. The suit kept the asteroid dust out, mostly, except for what transferred into the ship when I reentered, but that didn't keep me from feeling grimy. In a spacesuit, you sweat a lot more than they ever show in the tridees.

I climbed into the airlock, ready to head back to my little patch of human civilization on Ceres. The asteroid hosted a good ten thousand people at any given time. You could usually find someone to fulfill your needs, whatever they might be, either for free or for a chunk of your hard earned Ceries, the currency out here in the belt. I had a couple of each — free and paid companions — and the no-attachments life suited me just fine. Since Archer passed ... it was just better this way.

I'm not lonely.

The airlock lift rose into the belly of the ship, taking me with it, and stopped once it had a good seal. Air flooded the small space, and in less than a minute, the ascent resumed.

As I cleared the main cabin, I expected to see my visitor crumpled on the floor next to the lift, but his body was nowhere to be seen. "Dammit all to Phobos." *If that little bastard woke up and plundered my ship …*

"Welcome back, Cap." Rosie spoke in my ear.

"Where the hell is my captive?" I was feeling less than gracious.

"In the kitchen alcove."

"And you didn't think to tell me he'd woken up?" *Somebody* was due for a system overhaul.

"Sorry." She actually sounded sorry. "He seemed harmless enough."

I unlatched my helmet and was immediately assaulted by a strange smell. "Rosie, what in the stars-cursed void is that? Is one of the components on fire?"

"Just a little something I whipped up." The voice was chipper — a little *too* chipper.

I spun around to see my mystery man out of his suit, looking anything but *nearly dead*. He was even more handsome face to face than he'd looked through the visor.

"You — cooked?" My brain was struggling to catch up. He'd hung his suit, so at least he was trying to be courteous.

I'd expected to have to resuscitate him — my wildcatter friends would have had a field day with that one, but mouth to mouth isn't nearly as sexy as they made it look in *tridee* space adventure shows.

Flawless

I slipped out of my own bulky suit, hanging it up next to his, and experiencing a strange moment of déjà vu. Archer's ghost was always with me.

Taking a deep breath, I turned to face him again, aware how dingy my ship clothes were. I didn't do laundry all that often — even the ionic cleaner used a little precious water — and I'd been out on this run for six weeks.

My confusion must have been apparent, because the stranger blushed. "Sorry, didn't mean to step on your toes." He gestured at the wall near the kitchen nook. He'd figured out how to pop out the table and chairs there and had even found the magnetic plateware. "I hope you don't mind. I'm starving, I found your spice rack and thought I'd whip us up a little something. I've never even heard of half the things on it."

No wonder — a day or too stuck out on the surface of Eros was bound to make you hungry. I was still trying to wrap my head around the fact that there was a disgustingly handsome young man on my ship, making dinner for me. Using *my spices*.

"You're about out of cumin."

I frowned. That one bottle had cost me five hundred Ceries, which on Earth would have worked out to about a thousand bucks. "How much did you use?"

He smiled at me over his shoulder. "Oh, calm down. I just used a dash. Cumin is strong." He slid a plate in front of me, and my mouth began to water. Somehow he'd taken my mostly dried shipboard rations and made a plate a chef on Phobos would have been proud of.

As he slid onto the other chair, I looked up at him, my eyes wide. "Who are you?"

He extended his hand, his grin nearly undoing me. "Ferris, at your service. Fer, to my friends."

For an almost-dead man, he looked full of life. "What in the fucking void were you doing, trying to steal my score?" He wasn't going to get out of *that* by batting his pretty eyelashes. *Handsome or no.*

He blushed again and looked down at his plate. "Eat up. It'll get cold fast, and it's much better when it's hot." Setting an example, he dug into his own portion, filling his mouth with food so no more words could come out.

I growled. It *did* smell delicious. It was thick and sticky enough to stay on the plate, even in zero gee.

I took a forkful and sniffed at it suspiciously. My stomach rumbled, and my hand lifted the fork to my mouth without my volition.

An explosion of flavor coated my taste buds, and I moved it around with my tongue, trying to wring out every last bit of flavor. "Oh my stars, that's good." It tasted like chicken — yes, I'd had it on a couple of occasions after a big score, at *Piazzi*, the fancy restaurant on Ceres that the tourists frequented. Named for Giuseppe Piazzi, the astronomer who first discovered the almost-planet that I called home.

Ferris grinned. "I'm glad you like it. I've been cooking since I was five. My mother taught me all she knows, and she's a whiz at making do with whatever's on hand."

I took another bite. "Kid, you could open your own restaurant on Ceres to rival Piazzi with this."

He lit up like a homing beacon. "Mama said the same thing."

I swallowed the second bite and took a swig out of the drinking bottle he'd brought, and almost spit it out. "That's not water."

"Sorry." He turned beet red from neck to forehead. "I ... found your wine stash in the stores. I thought we should celebrate."

"Celebrate what?" I shut my trap, sure that I was going to be sorry I asked. "You weren't here to steal my score, were you?"

He shook his head. He stared at me, cocking his head as if he wasn't sure how to tell me what he'd obviously come all this way to say.

"Well? Spit it out." *How bad could it be?*

"I'm your son." He stared at me expectantly.

That was absolutely the last fucking thing I expected to come out of those lips. I dropped my fork. It wasn't nearly as dramatic as it sounds — it just floated away, depriving me of the dramatic gesture I'd hoped to make.

• • •

"You are *not* my son." I'd banished Ferris to the far side of the room, giving him a brush and a small canister vacuum and telling him to scrub both suits clean.

In the meantime, I'd taken up my station at the ship's deck, preparing for the flight back home.

"How can you know for sure?" At least he seemed to be taking his job seriously. He'd started on my suit, and half of it gleamed like new.

I grunted. "Because I don't sleep with women. Never have, never will. Except ..." There's been that one time, when I'd been drunk as a Martian miner at the end of my last school year. I'd never even known her name, and the whole thing was a blur. Still, it wasn't possible. Was it? It was just one time.

J. Scott Coatsworth

And cute or not, the boy was getting on my nerves. And he was a *boy*, even if his official age marked him an adult in the eyes of Common Law.

I ran through the preflight checks, which I would have done before eating, if I hadn't been shocked by my unexpected guest. I'd lift the *Swallow* off of Eros and haul in the can, and once it was secure, we'd set on our way to Ceres, where I could drop off his freeloading ass. If I didn't shove him out the airlock first — which was a lot harder with these one-man ships than you'd think.

My stomach rumbled, reminding me of the divine meal I'd just enjoyed, even if it had cost me almost a thousand Ceries between the cumin and the bottle of wine I'd been saving for a special occasion.

I felt his gaze bore into my shoulder blades. "She ... said you probably wouldn't remember. You were a bit drunk at the time."

I spun around to stare at him. "What?"

Fer — when did I start calling him that? — looked away quickly, busying himself with cleaning the other half of my suit. "It was right after school. Mamma said it was consensual. You met at a little bar called the —"

"Full Transit." I scratched my head. It was possible. "I ... it could have ... maybe." Holy fucking void, was this kid my son? "What is this? A *trideenovella*? Who is your mother, anyhow?"

"Dania Herralter. Didn't I mention that before?"

I stared at him, my mouth going dry.

The name hung in the air like a bit of sparkling regolith.

The kid I had cleaning space suits, the one I'd almost considered chucking off into space for messing with my can — yeah, I know how that sounds — was the Phobos-fucking son of the voids-damned Martian president.

• • •

Fer poked my shoulder. Again. "Say something."

"Give him a break, Cap." Rosie sounded happy, if that was possible. "I never figured you for a father."

"Me neither," I grumbled,. It was almost time — I had to take advantage of burn gravity. One of these days I'd make enough to buy a spinner ship and have fancy centrifugal "gravity" for the whole trip, but for now I was dependent on ship thrust.

Could I do this with the Martian President's son — and apparently my own — on my ship, staring at me like a lost puppy dog? *Yeah, I know. No dogs on Ceres.* But we had the *tridee* feed like everyone else, and the system wide web.

The *Swallow* had lifted away from Eros, a clean separation, and the last can was safely tucked into its well on the underside of the ship.

Our course was set, and in less than a week we'd be docking at Ceres, where I could hand this annoying passenger over to the local authorities to be returned to his mother. I just had to endure him until then.

"Seriously, talk to me."

I could feel Fer frowning, but I refused to engage. Instead I went over the course plot one more time.

"You look like you want to throw me out of the airlock. But you *like* me. I know you do." He sounded so earnest.

I can't say I wasn't a little tempted to ditch the little bastard. Who would know?

From what he'd told me, he'd come out here on his own in a scooter meant for short-range trips — somehow he'd managed to get a hold of my trip itinerary. He'd failed to secure the little craft properly, and it had drifted off while he was "exploring" the surface — the void knew where it was by now.

He slumped back into the second chair. Archer's chair.

I winced and said nothing. At least he'd gone quiet. I finished crosschecking our course. Satisfied we were on the right track, I sat back and exhaled heavily.

"I know who you are." He was staring at me.

I closed my eyes, wishing he would just go away. "Of course you do. You already told me you figured out I was your father, though you didn't tell me how." Had he bribed someone in the Ceres DNA Registry office? And how had an old mistake of mine end up becoming the freaking ruler of Mars? That would require an explanation. Someday.

"I know you're Valeriana Storm." He stared at me, daring me to deny it.

My heart raced, but I managed to stay calm on the outside. *I think.* I snorted with as much derision as I could summon up. "That's ridiculous. Do I *look* like Valeriana? The most glamorous drag queen this side of Luna?" I slipped my nail-polished fingernails under my knees, hoping he hadn't noticed.

"You're too late. I clocked your nails at dinnertime — not too many wildcatters wear polish. Or have a shit-ton of make-up stashed on board. Besides, I already knew." It was his turn to look away.

"You went through my stuff?" I knew I should have left him where I found him.

"He's got you, Cap." I could almost hear the snicker in her voice.

Flawless

"Shut up, Rosie."

Her laughter told me she didn't take my command too seriously.

Fer was grinning victoriously.

"Not that I'm admitting anything, but what would make you think that?" I thought back over our time together, wondering what had given me away. Sure, the platinum score would make my accountant back on Ceres very happy for a few months. But scores like that weren't a guaranteed thing. Valeriana had seen me through the lean times, the income she generated on the solar web keeping my account flush. But how had Fer figured it out?

"Honestly, I didn't believe it at first. You're so old." He said it without the slightest hesitation or hint of remorse.

"Hey, I could still throw you out of the airlock." *Maybe if I knocked him unconscious first ...*

He grinned. "But you won't."

"How do you *know*?" Over the years I'd cultivated a tough-guy look and attitude, totally at odds with Valeriana — who thanks to AI filters looked a good two decades younger than me. But the talent was all mine. No smart filter could manufacture that.

"I saw right through you the moment you came up through the airlock. You don't have a mean bone in your body." He paused, searching my face. "I think that's why my mother loves you."

Present tense. "You still haven't answered my question."

He leaned back in the chair. "You admiting you're her?"

"If I do, will you tell me?" He was going to find out soon enough, anyhow. I was starting to remember why I liked working — and living — alone.

"Sure." He grinned triumphantly.

I sighed. "I am, in fact, Valeriana Storm." I managed a regal half-bow in my chair. It felt strangely good to tell someone. Only the accountant knew, and I'd paid him off for his secrecy.

"Yes!" He clapped his hands like a five-year-old and punched the air. "I knew it!"

I said a prayer to the void for patience. "So *how* did you know? No one else has ever figured it out." I crossed my arms, ready for some kind of scientific explanation involving signal tracking and body scans.

"Mom told me."

I shook my head. "Try again. She knew me way before I was Valeriana."

"Honest to Mars, she knows. She saves all your broadcasts. I caught her watching them one day and asked her who you were." A wistful look came over his face. "I'd always wondered who my other parent was."

I looked away. "I'll bet this is a huge disappointment for you then. You were probably hoping for a Martian dreadnought commander, or some famous Redball player."

"Are you kidding me? This is *soaked*."

I wasn't up on the latest Mars slang, but given how dry Mars was, I figured that had to be good. Still, who in their right mind would be thrilled to have as their father a single, middle-aged man who spent all of his time out in the rocks, half of that dressed as a woman?

The rest of my brain was still playing catch up with the whole *I have a kid* thing. "But wait, how did your ... mother know?" I was also trying to wrap my mind around my one-time dalliance with the opposite sex having been with Dania *fucking* Herralter. I'd known her in school — she'd called herself Daniella back then — but we'd never been close.

"She said you had this thing you always did, the way you swayed your hips in a circle, one way, then the other, and then wrinkled your nose. She knew it was you the first time she saw you perform."

Shit. I have a tell. I guess she'd paid more attention to me than I did to her. Fortunately few people knew me well enough to put two and two together. "Okay, kid, you win. What do you want from me? I can slip you a wad of Ceries when we get home." Maybe if I paid him off, he'd just go away.

He shook his head. He was adorable ... in a different way, now that I knew he was my kid, but still ... he was probably used to getting his way with a mug like that. "I don't want your money."

"What then?" Did he plan to expose me? I'd always known that could happen. It wouldn't be the worst thing in the world, though losing my anonymity might come with a price. Right now I could come and go as I pleased without attracting undue attention.

"I want to see you perform."

I scratched my head. "You must have seen it before."

"Not up close and personal." He grinned, and his smile lit up the room.

Little fucker was getting to me. I didn't let anyone see me like that. My desire for secrecy aside, what Valeriana projected was one thing — finely honed, a mix of gods-given talent and inspired artistry and a hell of an expensive AI filter that turned me into the thing of beauty Fer — and his mother, apparently — idolized. "I'm not sure —"

"Pleeease?"

Somehow the little shit got to me with that extended entreaty. I glanced at the time — I did have a show to record, after all, and I was already late. I breathed in deeply, and then nodded. "On one condition."

"Name it." His eyes shown with excitement.

"You sit there silently for the whole show. You don't say a word. And you don't talk to me when it's over. Not until I'm Grayson Eck again. You understand?"

"It's okay. You don't have to be ashamed —"

"I am *not* ashamed." I leaned forward, forcing him back against the chair. "Do. You. Understand?"

Ferris gulped. "Yes, Sir. Ma'am. Sir."

"When I put on those clothes, I become Valeriana Storm. It's an illusion, but it overtakes me completely. And if you break it …"

He nodded, his face white. "Got it. I'll keep my mouth shut."

• • •

Half an hour later, we were on or way, the ship's thrust giving the *Swallow* partial gravity.

I had my make-up set up on the flip-down vanity in the bathroom nook of the ship. I'd taken a soothing ionic steam shower. In the charged mist, for a couple of blissful moments, I'd been able to forget I had a guest.

Until the mists cleared, and I caught him staring at me from across the room. He looked away quickly.

I had nothing to be ashamed of — I was in great shape for a man of fifty — but still, it was weird having company again.

I pulled my hair back tight and tied it behind my head, out of the way, tight enough that my face hurt.

Flawless

A dusting of nano-foundation smoothed my skin, making me look fifteen years younger — the sizzle reinvigorated my skin as the little buggers did their work. I bought only the good stuff, and paid extra to have it delivered anonymously in plain packages from Earth.

A layer of smart powder gave my face the *real but perfect* look that was trademark Valeriana, and a little contouring feminized my face, hiding my big nose and slimming my cheekbones. Each act took me another step away from Grayson, another inch toward Valeriana.

"Where did you learn to do all of that?" Fer's voice intruded on my world.

Valeriana's world. I held up my hand.

"Cap doesn't like any talking while he's becoming her."

Nice of Rosie, though now it was her voice distracting me.

"Oh, sorry." He really did sound apologetic.

I sighed. I wasn't quite Valeriana yet. I had a little wiggle room. "There are *tridee* tutorials on the solar web, if you look for them." Drag had been outlawed across much of Earth a century or so earlier, during the Dark Decade, but it had flourished in exile. When the bans had been lifted, one by one, it had come back with a vengeance, aided by new forms of make-up and even DNA re-profiling, if you wanted to take it that far. Me, I was happy with who I was. In and out of drag, though I took full advantage of filters.

I plucked my eyebrows and trimmed off a few hairs that had gotten longer than was proper for Valeriana's feminine wiles. A little make-up on my neck hid my Adam's apple. "Some queens do it all in post. I think that's cheating."

Though who's to say where the line is? Queens from the last century didn't have nanotech to aid their transitions, and they'd managed perfectly well. I said a quick prayer of thanks to Mother Ru, Valeriana's spiritual patroness.

"It's ... sticky, watching you become Val."

Sticky? I really needed to catch up on my Martian slang. "It's Valeriana. *Never* 'Val.'" Despite his annoying interjections, I decided I kinda liked having a live audience. This one time.

Picking up the wig I'd chosen, a flouncy red thing that I'd bought on Mars, I slipped it over my head, settling it in place. I'd told the clerk it was for my sister, who was going through treatment for a radiation tumor — a distressingly common if eminently treatable side effect of living on the red planet. *A little white lie.*

She'd winked at me knowingly. "Of course it is."

I stared at the porthole window in front of me that doubled as a mirror, seeing my transformed face floating in the stars. I stood up a little straighter, feeling Valeriana flow into me. I settled into her as the wig adjusted itself to fit the contours of my head.

I extended my nails using the shaper, and then polished them, choosing a juicy apple red that would be perfect for tonight's show. As the color flowed across each perfectly shaped oval, I began to hum one of her songs. *My songs.*

"Starchaser." More about a celebrity whore than a spaceship, but you could take it either way.

I finished my nails, closed my eyes, took a deep breath, and let it out smoothly.

I was Valeriana now. I'd felt her come over me, the shift in my energy from masculine to feminine. If you've never done drag, it's hard to explain what a profound change it is, or the confidence it gives you, confidence you carry back to your mundane life too.

I turned my chair around, taking another deep breath and letting her settle in.

"Don't you have to —"

My hand shot out, perfectly manicured nail up, to silence my audience. I wished I had a curtain, but I'd never needed privacy on my own ship before.

I turned my finger down toward the ground and gave him the universal sign for *turn around*.

"But I want to —"

Palm out this time, and he was silenced once again. Valeriana was very good with her hands.

I stared at my audience until he reluctantly turned to face the wall, and then dropped my pants unceremoniously.

I won't describe tucking in detail — the process by which a man goes from having those things between his legs to looking like he doesn't. Suffice it to say it involves some pushing inside, some pulling back, and ample taping to make sure the whole unwieldy appendage stays in place.

Being a drag queen is not for sissies.

Some of the *tridee* queens do all that in post too, but I've always considered that cheating. I need to *feel* like a woman. Valeriana demands it of me.

Satisfied, I pulled on my stockings, and then popped open the "closet" — a narrow space behind one of the ship's metal panels — where I kept Valeriana's clothing. I only had a few pieces — in this respect, I'd given into modern tech. The ship could only haul so much, and a holo dress allowed me to keep up with the latest fashions without breaking the bank — or the *Swallow's* weight allotment.

I caught Fer looking over his shoulder.

"Face to the wall, young man." Even my voice was different. And apparently commanding.

His head snapped back into place.

I slipped on the bland white dress and ran my fingers nimbly over the right sleeve to activate the fashion menu. Zeroing in on the red and gold palette, I settled on one that I would look stunning in — a red dress with a hand embroidered bodice in gold, barely puffed sleeves that suggested something a fairy-tale princess might wear, and a dramatic slit down the back that a sweet princess wouldn't be caught dead in.

The dress shimmered around me — void be damned, I was my own fucking fairy godmother. A pair of variable heels, painted red and gold at my whim, and I was ready for the ball.

"Boy." I clicked my nails.

Fer turned around, and I swear his jaw almost hit the deck. "Holy horizons. You're ... It's her." His eyes narrowed. "I thought the *tridee* put *on* ten pounds, not took it off."

"You should be careful how you talk to me, little boy. Grayson might not put you out an airlock for giving him mouth, but I have no such qualms." Hell of the nerve the boy had to call a woman fat to her face.

He swallowed hard. "Yes, ma'am."

"Better. Now sit down and let me put on my show."

He wasn't entirely wrong. Filters would slim my face — and the rest of me — and change my appearance enough to fool anyone who might use face-rec to try to figure me out. It wasn't vanity. Not exactly. More a matter of giving the audience what they wanted, and protecting Grayson in the process.

Flawless

"Rosie, my stage please." I waved my hand theatrically, and the center of the room rose a good three inches with a metallic *whir* and *clack*.

I stepped up onto it, and the rest of the ship went dark, a bright spotlight illuminating the center of the stage. The only other light came from the stars shimmering in the portholes that lined the cabin.

"What song, Valeriana?" Rosie knew me well.

"Starchaser." I closed my eyes, waiting for the music to swell, a dramatic piano entry blending seamlessly into an orchestral-thromb hybrid.

And when it did, I flew.

I never remember my sets afterward. It's almost a willful amnesia, as if my memory could never match the thrill, the grandeur of the real thing. But this time I knew I would.

For the first time, I had a live audience, even if it was just an audience of one. Somehow, that mattered. Someone — my son — was seeing me perform as myself, not the digitally enhanced version I fed to the solar web.

The music flowed through me as if I were just a conduit, its pulsing and flirting lifting me higher and higher like a lover. Verse followed stanza, pouring out of me like melodic water through a firehose, and Rosie captured it all to edit later.

The heavy beat shaking the entire ship until it seemed like it would burst.

I moved seamlessly from "Starchaser" to "Into the Flames," goosebumps springing up on my arms, hidden by my white elbow-length gloves. I *felt* the music in a way I hadn't in years, as Valeriana took me and made me her own. I sang all of my own songs, proud of my voice, not lip-synching like many queens these days. Though I could slay that too. I was Valeriana, and for a brief moment in time, I was a goddess.

Ferris's eyes were gleaming, a puppy grin plastered across his young face. I caught glimpses of him in the darkness when the spotlight glittered off my dress in just right way, lining his cheeks in gold.

At last it was time for a song I'd been preparing for this performance, for the ride home from Eros. Manicured hands splayed across my chest, I took another deep breath, a shiver running down my spine. "This last one is a little something new I've been working on the last few months. It's especially appropriate tonight, for reasons I can't share with you just yet. But maybe one day, you'll understand …" My eyes met his, and I felt seen for the first time in ages. "This is 'Lost'."

Floating through space
Stars my only guide
Waiting for your hail
Adrift in the dark night.

Lost is the last thing
You said to me.
"I'm lost
Without you."
Now you're gone …

Seven years without Archer. Seven long years since he'd been killed, taken from me far too soon. Now his face floated in the darkness before me.

I'd created Valeriana after he'd left me, because I needed *something* to do. Needed to have someone else. Maybe needed to *be* someone else.

She had never let me down.

Flawless

I closed my eyes, whispering the last words of the song.

I never should have let you go out ...
Alone.

I stood absolutely still as the spotlight faded. The last notes of the song drifted away, and when the ship's regular lighting came back up, she left me and took her power with her.

There was just me — Grayson — a poor, lonely middle-aged wildcatter in a red dress, staring at the void in my soul.

I pulled off my wig and began to cry, all of those emotions I'd walled away when Archer had been killed bursting out of me like water through a dam. I sank onto the platform, and Fer was suddenly at my side, easing me down to sit on the edge of the stage.

My make-up held against the onslaught, a perfect porcelain shell masking the turmoil inside.

Fer sat beside me and took my hand, and for a few moments he just let me cry. Grief filled me as completely as the music had earlier, wringing me out and leaving me dry.

"That was amazing," Fer said at last when my sobs had subsided. He reached over and snagged a rag from my make-up station. "Here."

I took it and dabbed my eyes, taking a ragged breath and trying to keep myself strong. "I'm sorry you had to see me like that."

"Don't worry about it. It looks like it was a long time coming." He took the damp cloth back and set it aside. "What happened to you up there? One minute you were soaring — I don't think I've ever seen such a magnificent performance. And then ..."

I owe you an explanation, don't I? I closed my eyes, unsure where to begin. "After your mother … after a whole succession of guys in my early to mid-thirties, I met Archer at a gallery on Ceres." I remembered him as he'd been then, flush with his success, selling half a dozen paintings to wealthy patrons. In a manic phase, though I didn't know it then. "He was so alive, so in his element, and I felt so out of mine. I didn't know art. I didn't know much of anything beyond spending months hopping from rock to rock and then weeks spending the spoils in bars and beds."

"He sounds amazing." Fer helped me up — not that I needed it, but I was still a bit strung out from the performance and all the released emotion — and guided me to my makeup station.

"He was. But he was tortured too, wracked by his own demons." I peeled off my false eyelashes, setting them back in their case. I'd have all this mess sorted and slotted before we finished our *out burn* phase and went back to weightlessness. "He was bipolar. They have drugs for that, and even genomic fixes now, but he always said they'd ruin the part of him that his art came from." I ran the dephaser over my cheeks, and the nanites in the foundation responded, letting go of my own aging skin so I could wipe them off with a clean cloth. "Still, that's not what killed him."

"What happened to him?"

I looked up, and our faces were close together, framed in reflection in the porthole. I hadn't seen it before, but I could now. He had something of me in him.

I stood and took off the dress and peeled off my stockings, hanging both up with a snap-hook. I'd give them a good cleaning later.

Flawless

I didn't care if Ferris saw me naked again. He'd already glimpsed a far more intimate part of me than my aging flesh. "We had three mostly good years together." I ripped off the tuck tape, needing to feel a little physical pain to dampen the emotional one.

Fer nodded, his eyes locked on mine, waiting for me to continue.

"When we were on the way home from a score on Psyche, halfway out to Jupiter, we were ambushed by pirates. Archer was outside at the time — we'd had a fight, over his meds, of all things, and he'd gone out to make some kind of repair. On a ship like this, there's nowhere else to go when you need a little privacy." He'd done it before, and he'd always come back inside. "When the *Raptor* found us — the pirate ship — he tried to make them leave — threatened them, even."

"Holy stars." Fer whistled.

"They holed his suit." I could still hear his last gasps over the com — they often kept me awake at night. I took a ragged breath, walling off the hurt. "I never saw him again."

"Fuck." Fer threw his arms around me and hugged me tightly, his warm body pressed against mine.

"Fuck indeed." Some slang never changed. It felt good to be held again — I'd forgotten how much I missed simple human touch. I'd long since made peace with losing Archer — or I thought I had.

When Fer finally let go, I kissed him on the cheek, and then turned back to put away all my bits and pieces, uncomfortably aware that he was staring at me. "What?" It came out more gruffly than I intended. *So much for not caring.*

"Would you ... teach me?" His gaze flicked to the dress, now a drab white sheet once more.

"Teach you what? Rock hopping?" I'd never considered having an heir. And his mother certainly wouldn't approve of her only son bouncing around all over the inner system. *I should send her a private comm to let her know he's all right.*

"No. This amazing thing you do. Drag." He said it like it was obvious.

I turned to stare at him. "You want to do *this*?"

"Sure. Why not? When you become her ... I've never seen anything so amazing."

You should see the rings of Saturn. "No. Absolutely not. Life out here is ... hard enough, without adding complications." The other rock hoppers — hell, half of Ceres — loved Valeriana. But they wouldn't love the man who became her. I wouldn't inflict that on my son. I started to get into the shower.

"Please?" He grinned, and his smile was dazzling. He'd make a beautiful queen, even without the filters.

I hardened myself to his charm. "Not in a million years."

"But Dad ..."

That stopped me in my tracks. "Don't call me that. I'm nobody's father." I stepped into the ionic steam shower again and slammed the door behind me, shutting him outside. I turned it on, just as the ship's thrusters kicked off. *Rookie mistake.*

The sudden loss of acceleration slammed me into the top of the small enclosure, and the world went black.

• • •

Flawless

I blinked.

The world was fuzzy, a series of white lights in a circle around me.

Angels? *Am I in heaven?* Not that I was a religious man, though 'catters tended to find religion in the belt after the void tried to take them out.

The glows slowly resolved themselves into cabin lights. I was laying on my back, strapped to my bunk, the memfoam holding me comfortably in place.

"You're awake." Fer's face drifted into view. "You feeling okay?" He was sipping on one of my bulbs of flavored water.

I raised a hand to my aching head. There was a goose egg there the size of an asteroid. "I ... think so. What happened?" I was wearing underwear — had Ferris put those on me?

"The ship thrusters stopped firing. You hit your head in the shower." He bit his lip. "Are we out of fuel?"

I unstrapped myself, sitting up and checking myself over. There was a small contusion on my shoulder — I'd probably rammed it against the ionic dispenser. But otherwise I seemed to be in good enough shape. "Nope, we're just in vector mode. We have all the speed we need to get back to Ceres. Space travel isn't like you see it in the *tridees*. You don't just jet about here and there, easy as you please."

His shoulders sagged with relief. "Good. I was afraid ..."

You'd be stuck out here with me until you died? Better not to know the rest of that sentence. "I'm a bit ripe. Rosie, why didn't you remind me?"

"You seemed very determined to take a shower, Cap. I thought you knew." Was it my imagination, or did she sound a little resentful at being blamed?

I sighed. Soon enough I'd be back in my flat on Ceres, and I could shut everyone out for a day or two. Or maybe a year. I sniffed myself. "Best get that shower —"

"Sorry, Captain Eck, but we've got something — or someone — inbound. Arrival in about seven minutes." Yeah, she was definitely annoyed with me. She never called me *Captain Eck*.

Ferris went white as a sheet. "Is it an asteroid?"

"Don't know, but I doubt it. Space isn't that crowded, and we know where most of the rocks are in the inner system." I slipped into the pilot's chair. "Rosie, what can you tell me about the incoming object?"

"One moment, Captain." Yeah. Frosty.

"I'm sorry, Rosie. I didn't mean to blame you."

"Thank you, Cap." Her voice was still terse, but at least she'd stopped calling me *captain*.

Ferris sank down into the second chair. "Are we in trouble?"

"Shush." I was reviewing the scan info as it came in, displayed as a 3D image above the deck. High metallic content. No spin. Very little reflected light. I knew what it was before Rosie responded.

"Looks like an unregistered ship. I'm not getting any response from their transponders."

"Fuck." Of all the bad-ass luck.

"What is it?" Ferris leaned forward to look at it with me.

"Pirates." I'd managed to steer clear of them for a few years — since Archer's death, I'd never ventured much past the orbit of Mars. They were either desperate or overly confident to hunt in the inner system.

Ferris frowned. "Think they're the same ones?"

Flawless

"Probably not." Hauls like mine were worth a lot of money on the black market, and it was easier to steal them than to mine them. There were a few different factions out there, and odds were it was someone other than Captain Davis — the man who had killed Archer.

I swung into action, starting with pulling on my shirt and pants. I had no intention of allowing those space thugs onto my ship, but if they did manage to board, I would *not* meet them dressed only in worn out briefs. "Rosie, initiate Protocol 1650."

"You sure, Cap?"

1650 was widely acknowledged as the year the pirate scourge had begun in the Caribbean — ancient history was another thing I had an affinity for.

"What's Protocol 1650?" Ferris stared at me as I gathered the little bits and pieces leftover from the show and stuffed them into cabinets. I would sort them out later.

"Rabbit and porcupine. You'll see." I'd spent a lot of money to implement a new ship defense after Archer's death.

Fer started to get up to help.

"Sit. We've got about thirty seconds left." I began to pull on my boots but realized it would take too long and stuffed them into a bin instead.

"Fifteen. Fourteen. Thirteen."

I made it back to my seat and strapped in with about three seconds to spare.

"Two. One. Zero. Protocol 1650 initiated."

The ship went dark. Not just on the inside, but the outside too, as a swarm of nanites crossed the hull, flipping her color from shining silver to matte black and raising a series of ominous looking bumps.

Pirates this far in-system were rare, but if they were enlarging their hunting grounds, I might do well to keep the new hull color.

"Rosie, any Belt Patrol ships nearby?" It was a faint hope. Space was big, even the space inside the orbit of Jupiter.

"Sorry, Cap. The closest is the *Trappist*. She's a day away by fastest course."

"Dammit." I took a deep breath, keeping myself calm. "Send them a tight beam message, advising them of a possible attack."

I looked over at Ferris in the darkness. "You okay, Fer?"

"I guess so." His silhouette turned to face me. "What … what happens now?" I could hear the quaver in his voice.

A single jet fired out some of our precious water, altering our course slightly. The water froze into a small cloud of ice, which would also hopefully confuse their scanners.

"Rabbit. We run in a different direction. If we're lucky, they lose track of us and go after easier prey."

"And if we're not so lucky?"

I shook my head. I'd had a couple of run ins before, farther out, but had never gotten past rabbit mode. "Porcupine. Let's hope that doesn't happen."

The *Swallow* drifted silently through the void on its new course, slowly edging away from the smooth path that would take us back to Ceres with the least amount of fuel. While that worried me, it had become secondary to the simple act of staying alive. Having enough fuel would mean nothing if we were blasted out of existence.

"Rosie, how close are they?"

Flawless

"Calculating ... they've gone dark too, Captain Awesome. Best guess based on last known position, 200 kilometers and closing. Estimated arrival in five-six minutes."

"Fuck Sirius." The brightest star in the heavens attracted more than its fair share of cursing.

"Maybe we've lost them?" The fear made Ferris's voice tremble.

"Maybe. But pirates are tenacious. I doubt I fooled them by changing course." Coming in hot, they'd have to brake at some point, and that would give them away. "I'm sorry you got stuck in the middle of this."

"I'm just glad you're not in it alone." He grinned, starlight illuminating his face just enough to let me see the gesture.

Maybe I wouldn't ship him back home right away. "When we get back to Ceres —"

"Intruder alert. They're here, Cap." The deck lit up, and I could see the intruder's jets burning in slowdown.

"Well shit. Rosie, deploy the spines."

"Aye aye, Captain." The ship vibrated.

"Spines?"

I swiped the deck to show a piece of the exterior of the ship. Those bumps were extending into long points, barely visible against the dark of the void in the backwash of light from the approaching ship. "Porcupine, remember?" The ship now resembles one of those puffer fish from Earth.

"Ah." He still sounded a little confused. Any discussion would have to wait, though. The pirates had arrived.

Their ship was about three times the size of my little craft, from what I could tell. It was an Arctus-class freighter, painted black like the *Swallow* now was, to better hide it in the darkness of the void. Emblazoned on the side of the hull was a white skull-and-crossbones.

I knew that ship. The *Raptor*. I shook with rage, with fear, with all the unresolved shit I'd been dealing with since Archer had been killed by these bastards. For just a moment, I wished I had something deadlier than *rabbit and porcupine*. "Dramatic." I growled. *I'll show you some drama.*

"That's her, isn't it. The ship that attacked you before." There was fear in Fer's voice, but anger too. Somehow that made me proud.

That killed Archer. "How did you know?"

"The look on your face. You went white as a comet."

I swallowed my fear. "Things will be different, this time." I was ready for them. *How quickly things changed.* "Rosie, contact our visitors."

"On what channel?"

Who the fuck knew what the official unofficial pirate channel was? "Try them all."

I reached over to squeeze Ferris's hand. "We'll get through this." I wasn't going to let those spacerats take my son from me too.

He nodded mutely in the darkness.

I wasn't sure if he believed me. Hell, I wasn't sure if *I* believed me.

"Communication achieved, Cap. Audio only."

I nodded. "Here we go." I held down the comm button — I liked to keep my communications on manual 'cause you never knew when you'd screw up and broadcast something you didn't mean to. *Like that time back on Phobos — well, never mind.* "Unknown ship, this is Captain Grayson Eck. Please respond."

Flawless

There was a long delay. Ferris and I glanced at each other nervously.

Finally the speaker flared to life. "Well, howdy there, Captain Eck. How nice to see you again, though it looks like your ship's gotten a bit of a retrofit since the last time we met." Davis's US southern accent was unmistakable, and the last thing you'd expect out here a few hundred million kilometers away from the homeworld.

I shuddered. That voice brought everything back — Archer's defiance, his last rasping breaths — my nails dug into my calf as I reminded myself to stay calm. The most important thing was to protect Grayson, Rosie and the Swallow. "What do you want, Davis?"

"That's *Captain* Davis. And what kind of tone is that to take with an old friend?" That last part practically dripped with sarcasm.

Two could play at that game. "We were never friends. Davis. What do you want?" *I'd like to see you freeze in the arms of Mother Void.*

A long sigh came over the comm. "We'd like to come visit y'all. Would you mind extending us a kindly welcome?"

"I'm afraid I can't do that." If I let them onto the Swallow, we were as good as dead. We might be anyway.

"And why is that, Captain Eck? Out here, all alone in the depths of space ... you really should make a stranger feel welcome." He sounded put-upon.

Welcome to my cargo. "I've already alerted the authorities to this ... unfortunate encounter, Mr. Davis."

"*Captain* Davis." I was starting to get to him. "And my comm officer assures me you've done no such thing." Though he sounded just a tiny bit less certain than before.

"Are you certain? What if, even now, a Cerian cruiser is bearing down on this little meeting?" I let go of the button. I wanted him to sweat.

"Cap, the *Trappist* hasn't responded yet." Rosie sounded more than a little worried now.

"I know that, and *you* know that. But our dear friend Davis can't know that. Not for sure." I pressed the button again. "*Captain* Davis. I'm a reasonable man. I know your ship is probably armed to the teeth, while you know relatively little about mine, beyond the fact that it's a Deneb-class ship, heavily modified. Do you really want to take a chance on boarding me?"

His reply came back a few seconds later. "I could just blast you out of existence and be done with it."

"Oh shit." Ferris's face had gone white enough in the darkness that he practically glowed.

I guess the time for pleasantries was over. "Hang on. We're about to give him what he wants. Or at least, mostly." No cargo was worth my life — or my son's. Or Rosie's for that matter.

I pushed the comm button. "You could. But seeing as we're *friends* ..." and I layered on about as much shade as a drag queen asteroid miner is capable of, "... how about we make a deal instead? You see, each of those spikes on my hull is a small heat-seeking missile. If you blow the *Swallow*," I paused to enjoy that delicious pun — Archer would have approved — "the *Raptor* will be collateral damage. I doubt even your vaunted defenses could stop them all. And if you try to disengage, I'll release them anyhow and you'll suffer heavy damage anyhow." *Either way, I'll take you down.*

Flawless

I didn't tell either Ferris *or* my new pirate friend that I'd called them "little dildos" when I'd first seen the designs. Some things were better left unsaid. *Precision missiles* sounded much more threatening.

Again the long pause.

I pictured that old KFC Chicken guy, rubbing his white beard, deep in thought. That's who he sounded like.

"What kind of deal?"

I had him hooked. "I'll give you a quarter of my platinum haul. You leave, I leave, and we all stay friends." *With friends like these ...*

"Surely, as such good friends, you'd give me at least half."

Good, he's still talking. Time for some theatrics. "Forty percent. That's my final offer." I let go of the comm button. "Rosie, light 'em up."

"Aye aye, Cap."

The viewport burst with light. I switched the view so that Ferris could see the exterior. Each of the spines/missiles now glowed an ominous red, the light radiating up the base in a repeating gradient pattern. *I know how to create drama.*

"So what do you say, Captain *Jack*?" I did love my old *flattie* films.

There was a long silence.

"What if he decides to try and board us anyway?" Ferris's gaze was glued to the viewport.

"Then we go boom." I closed my eyes. At least I'd be back with Archer if there was any sort of afterlife. "This isn't an easy life, kid." If we survived this, I'd drop him on Ceres and tell his mother to come pick the boy up — I couldn't bear to be responsible for his death, and she must be worried sick about him. *Might be nice to see her too, for old times' sake.*

The speakers flared again. "I'll accept your offer, but only because you seem like such an honorable and upstanding person."

I had him in a bind, and he knew it. If he could get out of this with his ship intact and his crew a little richer, he could spin it as a win to his crew.

"We have a deal then. Give me five minutes to release the canisters." It wouldn't take that long, but you always play for more time in hostage situations.

The response was immediate. "Three. And maybe we'll see each other out here again. *Friend*."

I shuddered. That sounded more like a threat. No one liked being humiliated and outplayed — self-styled pirates least of all. If we were lucky, the *Trappist* would get here in time to arrest the lot of them and send them to hard labor at the mines on Olympus Mons.

If not, I was sure he'd find a way around my counter threat by the next time our paths crossed. *Trouble for another day.*

"Rosie, prepare to release the cans … three, seven, eight and ten." The ones with the lowest grade metal, though they'd still be worth a fortune. I sighed. "Then prepare to fling the dildos at him and haul ass out of here."

"Dildos?" Ferris's face changed as comprehension dawned. "Oh!" He laughed, and then his brow furrowed. "But you said …"

"They're not missiles. Even on Valeriana's budget, I couldn't afford those. But they will create a little show to distract our new friend while we make good on our escape, and if we're lucky tie him down for a bit. Make sure you're strapped in." I checked my own belt. "Rosie, do we have enough fuel to make it back to Ceres?"

Flawless

"Calculating, Cap."

I waited nervously.

"Just enough to limp back home. You need bigger tanks."

I laughed. "Haven't had any complaints." Still, I'd think about it. Bigger tanks meant more fuel, but more fuel meant more weight meant a need for bigger tanks. Finding the optimum balance was key. I'd spec it out with Ronnie back in the garage on Ceres. They'd know what to do.

"Ready for release, Cap."

I thumbed the comm button. "Here you go, Captain Davis. Pleasure doing business with you."

Rosie let the designated canisters go, sending a clanking rumble through the *Swallow* as they drifted away behind the ship.

"Cap, The *Raptor* has a weapons lock on us."

Just what I expected. There was no honor among thieves. "Let 'em fly."

The dildos detached all at once, flashing a bright blue as they separated from our hull.

"What in the goddamned hell —"

I cut Captain Davis's voice off. "Hold on, Fer."

Rosie kicked the *Swallow* into high gear, burning fuel at a dangerously fast rate. We were forced back into our chairs as she accelerated away from the *Raptor*.

"Rosie," I forced it out from heavy-gee-pressed lungs. "Rear view."

For a second it showed only the blackness of space.

Then a shower of sparks bloomed across the screen in all the colors of the rainbow, the nanites shining brighter than the sun.

"What the hell was that?" Ferris was staring at the screen, mouth agape.

"Rosie and I call it a glitter bomb. All those nanites will be attracted to Captain Davis's hull, mucking it up and plugging the Raptor's missile tubes, communications antenna, and the like. He's dead in the water for a day, maybe two, until his crew can clean up the mess. With luck, he'll be scooped up by the BP before he's able to get things operational again."

Ferris laughed. "Oh my god, you're insane." Somehow he made it sound like a compliment.

I blew smoke off the tip of an invisible gun. "A lady always knows how to make an exit."

• • •

After five days of running silent, Ceres appeared before us at last, floating in the sparkling darkness of Mother Void. I sent a tight burst off to Ceres Control, requesting a landing and relating the attack that had nearly cost us our ship and our lives.

Fer and I had fallen into an easy companionship and work relationship. I showed him the basics of how to run the ship — he was a quick study, and by day three I was comfortable letting him take up the few tasks Rosie couldn't do.

He also sat with me on post-production edits on Valeriana's latest show before I sent it out to my relays on the web. It was my most popular yet, generating about seventeen million views by the time we reached port, and the resulting revenue made me feel just a smidgen better about losing forty percent of my platinum haul.

Maybe having the kid around wasn't such a bad thing after all. And maybe — just maybe — I should consider giving up the asteroid gig for good. Valeriana made me just as much money, if not more these days, without the hazards of rock hopping. And there was a certain Captain Davis out there who'd be gunning for me, next time I went out.

Besides, I wasn't getting any younger.

"Incoming call, Cap." Rosie's voice shook me out of my musings.

"Who is it?" Not Davis, I hoped.

"It's encoded, but it's coming from Ceres, or at least relayed through there. Do you want to accept?"

"Sure. Put it on the deck." I ran my hand through my unruly hair — time for a cut once I got home — and sat back in my chair to take the call.

Dania Herralter was suddenly staring at me, her face hovering over the deck. "Hello, Grayson."

I blinked. Now that I thought about it, I could see a little Ferris in her features. "Hello, Madame President. Though I think we used to know each other when you used a different name."

Her eyes narrowed. "Ferris told you. That little shit."

I laughed. "Yeah, he did. But you were Dania Black back then, right?"

"That was my *school name*. I didn't want everyone to know about my family. People treat you differently when they know you have money. And power."

That explained it. I didn't pay much attention to politics and had never made the connection. "I guess they would."

She frowned. "Is Fer all right?" Her voice took on a concerned mother's tone, real desperation masked in her voice.

"He's fine." I looked over my shoulder. "Fer, get your ass over here and say hello to your mother."

Fer slunk toward the deck like a six-year-old and sat in the other seat. "Hey, Mom."

"Ferris Grayson Herralter, if you ever pull a stunt like that again …"

He sank down into his chair, cowed. I was too — Dania was a force of nature.

My eyebrow raised at the middle name. "Why didn't you ever tell me?" The whole conversation had an air of the surreal about it. The President of Mars was talking to me on a secure line about our son. *Life is weird as shit.*

Her gaze returned to me. "You're a wildcatter. You're always hopping from one rock to another. What kind of life is that for a child?" She laughed unexpectedly. "Besides, you've been keeping a few secrets of your own, Valeriana."

"Fer already told me you knew." It was my turn to laugh at the frustrated expression on her face. "But how did *you* know?" I wasn't sure I bought Fer's explanation.

"I'm the President of Mars. I can find things out."

Something else occurred to me. "There's no lag on this call. You're on Ceres, aren't you?"

She smiled. "You always were a smart one. My agents tracked Ferris here, so we invented a trade mission to bring me out to this little ball of yours. It's impressive how it's changed in just the last ten years."

"It's not Mars, but it's getting there." I was proud of my current home.

"I don't want to go home." Fer spoke up for the first time since he'd sat down. His voice was full of resolve, no longer the little kid who'd sat down a moment before.

"Ferris … you've met your father. Now it's time —"

"You shouldn't have kept him from me."

I crossed my arms. "Total agreement on that."

Flawless

"And I'm sorry for that, Gray, but you have to admit, you weren't ready to raise a kid when we knew each other. I wasn't even ready."

She was right. But I couldn't let her get off that easily. "Still, you should have told me. Let me make the decision."

"My family never would have accepted you. As it was, they pressured me to … take care of it before Ferris was born."

"Still, you did commit a crime, Mom." Fer looked deadly serious.

"What crime?" we both said in unison.

"Grand theft semen." A grin split Fer's face, and then we were all laughing. The last bit of fear clenching my gut from our encounter with the *Raptor* dissipated.

Dania recovered first. "Still, it's too dangerous for him to stay with you. After your run-in out there with pirates …"

"How —"

"President of Mars, remember? You did call on one of our cruisers for help. You'll be happy to know that they apprehended the pirates, and the sale of three cannisters of platinum will be credited to your account."

That did make my day, The thought of *Captain* Davis in a red jumpsuit … "I still haven't heard an apology."

She sighed. "I'm sorry I kept you two apart. I was afraid Ferris would run after you, drawn in by the glory of being a wildcatter, roaming the belt." She held out a hand, decorated with a series of red rings. "And look. I was right."

Glory? She'd watched too many *tridees*. I took a deep breath, and then actually thought about what she was saying. *A guy can change if he tries hard enough.*

I liked my privacy. I liked getting away from the world — even such a small world as Ceres. And I did love my freedom. But the run-in with the *Raptor* had reminded me how dangerous it could be out there. And I suddenly had a good reason to try a different course.

"Let the boy stay with me for a bit, Dania." The words were out of my mouth before I knew it, but they were from my heart.

"What?" Fer's head whipped around to look at me.

"No!" Dania said at the same time.

"Why not? Look, he's a smart kid — smart man — and he's old enough to decide these things for himself." Twenty years old. *Great void, how old did that make me?* "Besides, you owe us the time to get to know each other better."

Her eyes flicked from me to him and back. "It's too dangerous."

Time for my ace in the hole. "What if I gave up wildcatting?" *For now.*

"You'd do that?" This time they both spoke together.

"Yeah. I mean, the kid's a pain in the ass. You really should have raised him better." I winked at Fer. "But I do kinda like him."

And having a full water shower — Ceres was flush with the stuff — every night didn't sound half bad. "Besides, I think it's time for Valeriana to make her homerock debut." It would make my life immeasurably simpler, not having to hide her anymore.

Ferris grinned. "You could teach me how to do *that*, too."

Dania shook her head. "You're *not* making my son into a drag queen."

I laughed. "One thing at a time. Can we agree that Fer can stay with me for, let's say, six months, and revisit things then?"

Flawless

Dania rolled her eyes. "I suppose it wouldn't be the worst thing in the world to have his father in his life. Assuming you keep your promise and give up the rock hopping."

I raised three fingers. "Martian scout's honor. I'm not selling the *Swallow*, though."

"I wouldn't expect you to."

I swear I heard Rosie sigh with relief.

Dania nodded curtly. "Sounds like a flawless plan." She looked up at someone offscreen. "I have to go. There's a meeting on the books with the mayor of Ceres in five, and I don't want to keep them waiting. How soon are you getting in? We can get dinner at Piazzi and discuss this further."

"Sounds good. See you then." I grinned. I knew I'd won.

Her image winked out of existence over the ship's deck.

"Rosie, how long till we arrive in port?"

"We'll be home in two hours and thirty-seven minutes, Cap."

Home. That sounded right.

AUTHOR'S NOTE

A FEW YEARS BACK, I had an idea for a short story about a wildcatter — an asteroid prospector who thrives on being alone.

I added it to my list of story ideas, and there it sat for a long time, until last year, when I was looking for a short story idea to work on. Being a huge *Drag Race* fan, I was struck by sudden thought. How cool would it be to write about a drag queen in space? Especially one who's a rough redneck asteroid miner by day?

I sat down and wrote Greyson Eck's story, and submitted it to all the major SFF magazines. None of them wanted it. I was getting ready to publish it in an upcoming short story collection of my own when Steven Radecki, the publisher at Water Dragon Publishing, asked if I had any short stories laying around that I might want to submit for his Dragon Gems program. I sent this one over, and the rest is history.

I worked with Kelley York on the cover, and am thrilled with how it came out.

Valeriana Storm is old school (thanks to my friend Alexis Kennedy for the great drag name). While she doesn't eschew modern technology, she believes drag should be real, not something you paint on in post with software. And yes, tucking is still very much a thing in the 23rd century.

In recent years, drag has gotten a lot of flack from certain quarters, with inflammatory and bogus claims that drag queens prey on children. Nothing could be farther from the truth.

Flawless

I wanted to tell a different kind of story about this amazing art form. Drag is all about finding out who you really are. When Grayson meets his son, drag empowers them both, and he owns up to who he is for the first time with another human being. That's what drag is.

As RuPaul says, "If you can't love yourself, how the hell you gonna love someone else?"

ABOUT THE AUTHOR

J. Scott Coatsworth writes stories that subvert expectations, that seek to transform traditional science fiction, fantasy, and contemporary worlds into something new and unexpected. His writing, whether romance or genre fiction (or a little bit of both), brings a queer energy to his stories, infusing them with love, beauty and power and making them soar. He imagines a world that could be and, in the process, maybe changes the world that is, just a little.

A Rainbow Award-winning author, Scott's debut novel, *Skythane*, received two awards and an honorable mention. With his husband, Mark, he runs Queer Sci Fi, QueeRomance Ink, Liminal Fiction, and Other Worlds Ink. Scott is also the committee chair for the Indie Authors Committee at the Science Fiction and Fantasy Writers Association (SFWA).

ALSO BY THE AUTHOR

THE DRAGON EATER
THE THARASSAS CYCLE: BOOK ONE

Raven's a thief who just swallowed a dragon.

A small one, sure, but now his arms are growing scales, the local wildlife is acting up, and his snarky AI familiar is no help whatsoever.

Things are about to get messy.

THE GAUNTLET RUNNER
THE THARASSAS CYCLE: BOOK TWO

A guard and a thief. What could go wrong?

Aik has fallen hopelessly in love with his best friend. But Raven's a thief, which makes things ... complicated.

Things were messy before ... but now they're much, much worse.

THE HENCHA QUEEN
THE THARASSAS CYCLE: BOOK THREE

Silya finally comes into her own, but will she be enough?

Silya finally has everything she always wanted: She's the Hencha Queen, head of the Temple, and is mastering her newfound talents. So why does the world pick now to fall apart?

Forget messy. Things just got apcalyptic.

Available in hardcover, trade paperback, and digital editions
Water Dragon Publishing
waterdragonpublishing.com

YOU MIGHT ALSO ENJOY

ARE ONE
by Michael A. Clark

What if a legend walks among us, but goes unnoticed?

What if a myth is reborn, but the world yawns in reply?

HAMM AND MEGS
by Gary Battershell

When Megan decided to go on a camping trip with her two college roommates, she had no idea that she would find herself involved in an alien plot to conquer Earth.

THE PAPERCLIP WAR
by Mikko Rauhala

After a nebulous Enemy destroys Earth, the remnants of humanity settle on Mars. Not only does this civilization survive, but they thrive, creating advancements for the rest of the solar system.

Available in trade paperback, and digital editions
Water Dragon Publishing
waterdragonpublishing.com

Milton Keynes UK
Ingram Content Group UK Ltd.
UKHW012117020524
442050UK00001B/26